Alligators

Edited by Katie Gillespie

LIGHTBOX
openlightbox.com

Go to
www.openlightbox.com,
and enter this book's
unique code.

ACCESS CODE

LBE79494

Lightbox is an all-inclusive digital solution for the teaching and learning of curriculum topics in an original, groundbreaking way. Lightbox is based on National Curriculum Standards.

STANDARD FEATURES OF LIGHTBOX

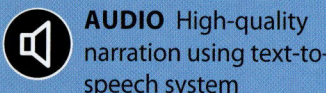 **AUDIO** High-quality narration using text-to-speech system

 ACTIVITIES Printable PDFs that can be emailed and graded

 SLIDESHOWS Pictorial overviews of key concepts

 VIDEOS Embedded high-definition video clips

 WEBLINKS Curated links to external, child-safe resources

 TRANSPARENCIES Step-by-step layering of maps, diagrams, charts, and timelines

 INTERACTIVE MAPS Interactive maps and aerial satellite imagery

 QUIZZES Ten multiple choice questions that are automatically graded and emailed for teacher assessment

 KEY WORDS Matching key concepts to their definitions

Copyright © 2016 Smartbook Media Inc. All rights reserved.

Animals of North America

Contents

Lightbox Access Code	2
Meet the Alligator	4
All about Alligators	6
Alligator History	8
Alligator Habitat	10
Alligator Features	12
What Do Alligators Eat?	14
Alligator Life Cycle	16
Encountering Alligators	18
Myths and Legends	20
Alligator Quiz	22
Key Words/Index	23
Log on to www.openlightbox.com	24

Meet the Alligator

Alligators are a type of animal known as a reptile. Reptiles are cold-blooded animals that have scaly skin and **vertebrae**. Alligators can live on land and in water. They have long bodies and very strong jaws.

Alligators have different ways of keeping their body at the right temperature. If an alligator wants to cool down, it enters the water. If it wants to get warm, it sits in the sunlight on land. At night, most alligators stay in the water because the water has been warmed by the Sun all day.

Alligators are very good swimmers. They often spend a great deal of time floating just beneath the surface of the water. They hold out their legs on either side of their body for balance.

Adult alligators are black or olive brown with a white underside.

All about Alligators

Alligators come from a family of reptiles called crocodilians. Crocodilians live both in water and on land. They have long bodies and short legs. Their skin is made of thick scales.

Many people confuse alligators with crocodiles. Both are crocodilians, but they have differently shaped heads. Alligators are usually only found in fresh water. Crocodiles can live in both fresh and salt water.

Crocodile Skull

Alligator Skull

Alligator Habitat
States with the Highest Alligator Populations
1 Insta-Gator Ranch & Hatchery
2 St. Augustine Alligator Farm Zoological Park
3 Everglades Alligator Farm

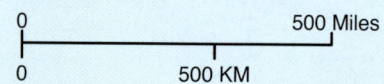

Alligators in America

Alligator History

The earliest crocodilians appeared on Earth about 84 million years ago. They came from a group of dinosaurs called archosaurs. The word archosaur means ruling reptile.

Crocodilian **ancestors** walked upright on two legs. As they spent more time in the water, they began to walk on all four legs with their bellies to the ground. This helped them move more easily through the water.

At this time, many species of crocodilians lived on Earth. Today, only 23 species of crocodilians still exist. They belong to five groups called crocodiles, caimans, gharials, false gharials, and alligators.

Alligators, crocodiles, and birds all were related to the archosaur.

Alligator Timeline

84 Million Years Ago
Ancient relatives of the alligator called archosaurs first appear on Earth.

66 Million Years Ago
Ancestors of American alligators survive the extinction of the dinosaurs.

40 Million Years Ago
Alligators crossed the Bering Sea land bridge from Asia into North America.

1568
The first recorded English use of the term *el lagarto* appears. The name comes from a Spanish word meaning "lizard."

1950s and 1960s
Alligators are hunted almost to the point of extinction.

1987
The alligator population increases. They are taken off the **endangered** species list.

Today
American alligators are still being protected. They are listed as a threatened species.

Alligators 9

Alligator Habitat

Alligators live in fresh water. They are very protective of their territory and can move quickly. Large alligators prefer to live alone, though small or younger alligators often share a habitat. A safe distance from an adult alligator is about 35 feet (11 meters).

American alligators live throughout the southeastern United States. They are found mostly in Florida and Louisiana. They also live in Alabama, Texas, North and South Carolina, Mississippi, Arkansas, and Oklahoma.

Alligators thrive in warm climates. They cannot tolerate freezing temperatures. On cold days, alligators will hide in their burrows.

 Adult alligators **weigh more than a piano**.

An alligator's teeth are **hollow**.

Alligators can live up to **50 years** in nature.

Alligators have **no** vocal chords.

Alligators can only stay in salt water for short periods because they do not have salt glands. They live in fresh water rivers, swamps, lakes, ponds, creeks, and canals.

Alligator Features

Alligators have many features that help them survive in nature. For instance, they have a large flap of flesh in the back of their mouth. It blocks water from getting into the alligator's lungs, keeping the animal from drowning.

SCALES
The skin of an alligator is thick and full of scales. It acts as **armor** to help protect the alligator from other animals.

TAIL
Alligators have strong tails that help them move in the water. They use their tails to push themselves out of the water with one big push.

LEGS
Alligators have short, powerful legs. On land, they can run very quickly in short bursts.

EYES
As **nocturnal** animals, alligators can see very well at night. This helps them see their **prey** when they hunt at night. Alligators can see colors.

NOSE
An alligator's nose is found on top of its snout. This is so that it can breathe while its body remains under the surface of the water.

JAWS
Alligators have strong jaws and sharp teeth. They crush animals with their powerful jaws.

Alligators 13

Alligators store fat in their bodies. If needed, they can live for up to two years without eating.

14 **Animals of North America**

What Do Alligators Eat?

Alligators are **carnivores**. They eat fish, small animals, such as turtles, and large animals that come near the edge of the water where alligators live. An alligator can hunt prey much larger than itself, such as deer.

Alligators wait in the water until their prey comes close to them. Then, they attack, grabbing the animal and pulling it into the water. Once the animal is in the water, the alligator crushes it between its massive jaws.

To prey on fish, alligators lie in shallow water with their mouths open. They wait for the fish to swim nearby. Then, alligators snap up the fish in their jaws.

Alligators have very strong jaws. They use them to eat animals with bones or hard shells, such as turtles.

Alligator Life Cycle

The alligator life cycle begins on land. Alligators make their nests out of plants and mud. They are careful when picking a site for their nests.

Nesting

Alligators lay their eggs in the nest and **incubate** them for two to three months. Whether the eggs turn out to be male or female depends on the temperature of the nest. If the temperature of the nest is 93° Fahrenheit (34° Celsius) or higher, the eggs will become male alligators. If the nest is 86°F (30°C) or less, the eggs will become female alligators. Any temperature in between this will make a mixed group of male and female **hatchlings**.

Hatchlings

As the shells of the eggs begin to break, the hatchlings start to croak. Carrying up to 20 eggs at once, the mother places the hatching shells in water and washes them. The hatchlings do not look much like alligators yet. They are lighter in color than adult alligators and have striped tails and bodies.

Adults

An adult American alligator weighs about 800 pounds (360 kilograms). Females are smaller than males. The average female grows to about 8.2 feet (2.6 m). Males average about 11.2 feet (3.4 m) long. Once alligators enter adulthood, they live alone.

Juveniles

As hatchlings grow, their skin gets darker. They begin to **communicate** by making high-pitched grunting noises. Alligators start mating when they reach a certain length. This length is different for each type of alligator.

Alligators 17

Encountering Alligators

At one time, the American alligator was an endangered species. There were no rules to protect alligators from being hunted. Since the late 1970s, laws have been put in place to protect alligators. Now, they are listed as a threatened species instead of endangered.

There are many alligator farms in the United States. Here, alligators can be viewed from a safe distance. If you encounter an alligator in nature, leave the animal alone and back away slowly.

Alligators should never be approached. People should not try to touch or feed an alligator. If you encounter an alligator in the backyard, rush back inside the house, shut the door firmly, and immediately contact the local emergency number for help.

One alligator can go through up to 3,000 teeth in its lifetime.

Alligators are the official state reptile of Florida.

Female alligators lay up to 90 eggs at a time.

Alligators have two different sets of eyelids.

Animals of North America

In many states, it is illegal to feed and touch alligators.

Alligators 19

Myths and Legends

Alligators have been on Earth longer than humans. They have been part of legends and folk tales for hundreds of years. These legends come from different parts of the world.

In China, there are many myths about dragons. Some of these myths describe dragons in a way that makes them seem similar to alligators. The ancient Chinese said the dragon was a reptile with horns and sharp teeth, much like an alligator.

The Choctaw American Indian group have a myth about a man who met an alligator in the forest. The man helped the alligator. In return, the alligator taught the man how to become a great hunter.

Chinese dragons were considered by many to be the king of animals.

20   Animals of North America

The Alligators in the Sewer

Some legends about alligators are quite new. One of the most popular myths is about alligators in the sewer. It takes place in New York City.

A family from New York City went on holiday to Florida. The family visited an alligator farm and saw baby alligators. The children found the baby alligators so cute that the parents decided to buy each child an alligator as a pet.

When the family returned to New York, the children enjoyed playing with the little creatures. As the alligators started to grow, they were not as cute. The children did not want to play with them as much.

One day, one of the baby alligators bit the youngest child. The father foolishly decided to flush the alligators down the toilet. Today, some people still believe that alligators live in the sewers of New York City.

Alligator Quiz

1 What type of animal is an alligator?

2 Where are alligators found in the United States?

3 How are alligators different from crocodiles?

4 Where do alligators lay their eggs?

5 What is a safe distance to stand from an alligator?

6 What determines an alligator's gender?

7 When did the earliest alligators appear?

8 What kind of water do alligators live in?

9 What helps alligators move through the water?

10 How many teeth can an alligator go through in a lifetime?

Answers: 1. Reptile 2. Florida, Alabama, Oklahoma, North and South Carolina, Texas, Arkansas, Louisiana, and Mississippi 3. Alligators have differently shaped heads and usually live only in fresh water. 4. In nests of mud and plants 5. 35 feet (11 m) 6. Temperature 7. 84 million years ago 8. Fresh water 9. Their strong tails 10. Up to 3,000

Key Words

ancestors: animals from the past that are related to modern animals

armor: a hard covering

carnivores: animals that have a diet of mostly meat

communicate: to exchange information

endangered: under threat of completely disappearing from Earth

hatchlings: newly hatched animals

incubate: to keep eggs warm

nocturnal: most active at night

prey: an animal hunted for food

vertebrae: small bones in the spine

Index

archosaur 8, 9

crocodilians 6, 8

eggs 16, 18, 22

endangered 9, 18

fresh water 6, 10, 11, 22

hatchling 16, 17

jaws 4, 13, 15

nest 16, 22

prey 13, 15

reptile 4, 6, 8, 18, 20, 22

scales 6, 12

LIGHTBOX

➕ SUPPLEMENTARY RESOURCES

Click on the plus icon ➕ found in the bottom left corner of each spread to open additional teacher resources.

- Download and print the book's quizzes and activities
- Access curriculum correlations
- Explore additional web applications that enhance the Lightbox experience

LIGHTBOX DIGITAL TITLES
Packed full of integrated media

VIDEOS

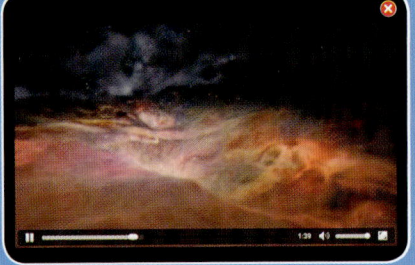

INTERACTIVE MAPS

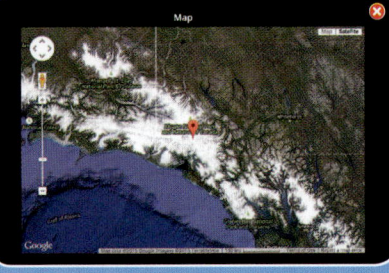

WEBLINKS

SLIDESHOWS

QUIZZES

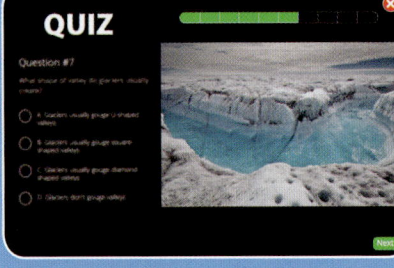

OPTIMIZED FOR
- ✓ TABLETS
- ✓ WHITEBOARDS
- ✓ COMPUTERS
- ✓ AND MUCH MORE!

Published by Smartbook Media Inc.
350 5th Avenue, 59th Floor New York, NY 10118
Website: www.openlightbox.com

Copyright © 2016 Smartbook Media Inc.
All rights reserved. No part of this publication may be reproduced, stored in a retrieval system, or transmitted in any form or by any means, electronic, mechanical, photocopying, recording, or otherwise, without the prior written permission of the publisher.

Library of Congress Control Number: 2015942495

ISBN 978-1-5105-0096-9 (hardcover)
ISBN 978-1-5105-0097-6 (multi-user eBook)

Printed in the United States of America in Brainerd, Minnesota
1 2 3 4 5 6 7 8 9 0 19 18 17 16 15

062015
030615

Editor: Katie Gillespie
Designer: Mandy Christiansen

Every reasonable effort has been made to trace ownership and to obtain permission to reprint copyright material. The publisher would be pleased to have any errors or omissions brought to its attention so that they may be corrected in subsequent printings. The publisher acknowledges Getty Images and iStock as its primary image suppliers for this title.

Animals of North America